what is happening in the pictures.

Each child is an individual and develops at his own pace. Be patient if your child is struggling with words. It is more important to value what he *can* do than to become anxious about progress. The learning steps will all be taken in time, with your help. At the back of this book you will find suggestions on how to make the best and fullest use of this book.

* In order to avoid the clumsy 'he/she', the child is referred to as 'he'.

Geraldine Taylor is a national broadcaster, writer and authority on involving parents in their children's education. She contributes on this subject regularly to magazines for parents.

Working with schools in Avon, Geraldine helps parents and teachers to act in partnership to benefit children's learning confidence and family happiness.

Acknowledgment:
Front endpaper and front cover illustration by Lynn Breeze.

British Library Cataloguing in Publication Data
Taylor, Geraldine
    Talkabout animals.
    1. English language—Readers—For pre-school children
    I. Title   II. Smallman, Steve   III. Series
    428.6
    ISBN 0-7214-1096-0

Published by Ladybird Books Ltd Loughborough Leicestershire UK
Ladybird Books Inc Auburn Maine 04210 USA
Printed in England

animals

written by GERALDINE TAYLOR
illustrated by STEVE SMALLMAN

Ladybird Books

Old Macdonald had a farm...

Can you sing
the song?

Look at all the animals
that live there.

Can you make a noise
like each of these animals?

6

7

These animals live in
the country.

Do you know their names?
Have you seen any of them?

Look closely –
what can you see?

Can you tell the story of the duck family?

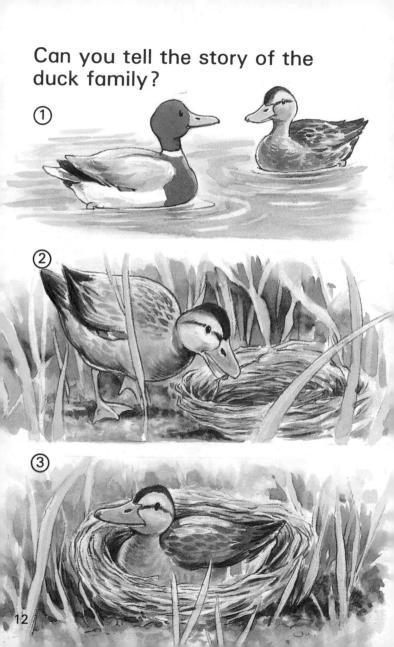

① ② ③

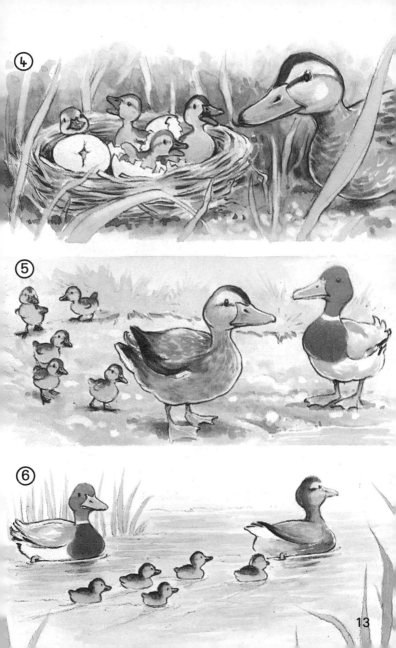

Count the jungle animals.

1

2

3

4

5

Now look at the next page.

15

Can you find the animals again?

Did you find all five snakes?

What do these animals eat?

Can you find
another...

like this

and this

and this?

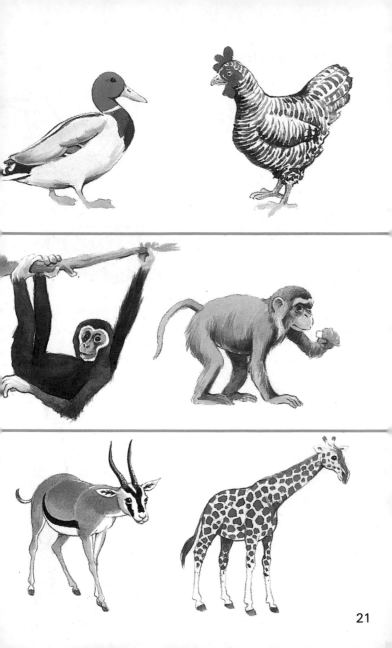

21

If you were a bird...

...what colour would *your*
feathers be?

Can you match each animal to its shape?

Some animals are awake at night.

Some sleep through the winter.

Some animals live where it is very cold...

...and some live where
it is very hot.

Many creatures live in the sea.

Can you find the jellyfish?

Here are some animals with their babies.

How do these animals move?

Can you jump like a kangaroo?

Can you tell the story about the hare and the tortoise?

Which picture
matches this
one…

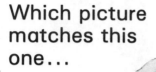

and this one…

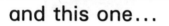

and this one?

Can you tell the story of the very long dog?

Here are some animal rhymes.
Can you say them?

Two little dicky birds,
Sitting on a wall;
One named Peter
The other named Paul.
Fly away, Peter!
Fly away, Paul!
Come back, Peter!
Come back, Paul!

Little Bo-Peep has lost her sheep
And doesn't know where to find them;
Leave them alone and they'll come home,
Bringing their tails behind them.

Hey diddle diddle,
The cat and the fiddle,
The cow jumped
over the moon;
The little dog laughed
To see such fun,
And the dish ran away
with the spoon.

Hickory, dickory, dock,
The mouse ran up the clock,
The clock struck one,
The mouse ran down,
Hickory, dickory, dock.

talkabout animals

Young children respond to the enthusiasm adults bring to discussions with them. If you are eager to talk and listen, your child will be, too. Don't feel self conscious about bringing that all important excitement and fantasy to conversations with your child.

Ladybird talkabout books are designed to encourage children to talk about their everyday experiences. There are suggestions on each page which will help you and your child to talk imaginatively about animals, both in the book and in the world around us.

Talking about picture stories helps children to understand that things happen in an order, with a 'before' and an 'after'. Use the pictures to tell the story yourself, first. Make the story special by, say, choosing a name for the very long dog, and wondering what